THE BEST JOKES FOR

YEAR OLD KIDS!

OVER 250 FUNNY JOKES!

With over 250 really funny,
hilarious Jokes,
The Best Jokes For 10 Year Old Kids!
promises hours of fun for
the whole family!

Includes brand new, original and
classic Jokes that will have the kids
(and adults!) in fits of laughter
in no time!

These jokes are so funny it's going
to be hard not to laugh!
Just wait until you hear the
giggles and laughter!

Books by Freddy Frost

The Best Jokes For 6 Year Old Kids
The Best Jokes For 7 Year Old Kids
The Best Jokes For 8 Year Old Kids
The Best Jokes For 9 Year Old Kids
The Best Jokes For 10 Year Old Kids
The Best Jokes For 11 Year Old Kids
The Best Jokes For 12 Year Old Kids

To see all the latest books by Freddy Frost just go to **FreddyFrost.com**

Contents

Funny Q & A Jokes!

How did the butcher introduce his
new girlfriend to his family?
Meet Patty!

What did the bee say when he
got home from work?
Honey, I'm home!

What did King Kong say when he
found out his sister had a baby?
Well, I'll be a monkey's uncle!

Why did the elephant decide to leave the circus?
He was sick and tired of working for peanuts!

What did one snowman say to the other?
Can you smell carrots?

If a cat ate lots of coins what would you have?
Money in the kitty!

Why did the football coach go to the bank before the big game?
To get his quarterback!

Where do computers party all night?
The Disk O!

What did one coin say to the other coin?
Together, we make cents!

What would Superman be called if he lost all his super powers?
Man!

Why did the lady wear a helmet to dinner?
She was on a crash diet!

Why did Robin stop playing cricket?
He broke his bat, man!

How did the math teacher know the girl was lying?
Her story didn't add up!

Why did the gorilla have huge nostrils?
She had big fingers!

What do you call a bear in the shower?
A drizzly bear!

What position does a monster
play on a soccer team?
Ghoulie!

What did the bees do when they moved
into their new house?
Had a house swarming party!

Why was the big rock braver than
the little rock?
He was boulder!

Where did the baby fruit have
a sleep?
In an apri-cot!

How did the smartest student
get to school?
On her scholar-ship!

What does a spider wear on
her wedding day?
A webbing dress!

What did the crab say to
the big wave?
Long time no sea!

Why are dalmatians no good
at hiding?
They are easy to spot!

Where did the alien get a coffee?
Starbucks!

What do you call a boy who is
a long way away?
Miles!

If you are really cold and grumpy
what do you eat?
A brrrgrrr!

How did the Vikings send a
secret message?
Norse code!

Why did the T-Rex sit next to
the fire?
He was a cold 'saur!

Where do fish sleep?
In their river bed!

How do you stop a bull
from charging?
Take away its credit card!

Why are beavers always
on the internet?
They never log off!

What did the picture say
to the window?
Help! I've been framed!

What did the big cow say to
the small cow?
Moooooove over!

What kind of button won't undo?
A belly button!

What did Kermit the Frog and Alexander the Great have in common?
The same middle name!

Why did the photo end up in jail?
It was framed!

Why did the cows all go
to Broadway?
To see the mooosicals!

Why are opera singers fun friends?
They leave you on high note!

What do you call a really cold dog?
A Pup-Sicle!

Funnier Knock Knock Jokes!

Knock knock.

Who's there?

Earl.

Earl who?

Earl be very happy when you let me in!

Knock knock.

Who's there?

Andrew.

Andrew who?

Andrew a very nice picture of you.

Do you want to see?

Knock knock.

Who's there?

Harry.

Harry who?

**Harry up!
I need to pee!**

Knock knock.

Who's there?

Diesel.

Diesel who?

**Diesel be the best
holidays ever!**

Knock knock.
Who's there?
Eddy.
Eddy who?
Eddy body home?
I ran out of food!

Knock knock.
Who's there?
Havana.
Havana who?
I'm Havana great time out here!
Want to join me?

Knock knock.

Who's there?

Amanda.

Amanda who?

Amanda repair that window you broke wants to charge me $200!

Knock knock.

Who's there?

Fixture.

Fixture who?

Fixture doorbell. That will be $100 thank you!

Knock knock.
Who's there?
Jimmy.
Jimmy who?
Jimmy 2 seconds and I will tell you all about it!

Knock knock.
Who's there?
House.
House who?
House about letting me in before I fall asleep!

Knock knock.

Who's there?

Furry.

Furry who?

Furry's a jolly good fellow!

Knock knock.

Who's there?

Flea.

Flea who?

I knocked Flea times!
Why didn't you answer?

Knock knock.
Who's there?
Despair.
Despair who?
**Despair tyre is flat!
Better get it fixed!**

Knock knock.
Who's there?
Detail.
Detail who?
**Detail of your cat is so fluffy I
want to tickle your chin with it!**

Knock knock.

Who's there?

Juicy.

Juicy who?

Juicy the news?

Grandpa won the marathon!

Knock knock.

Who's there?

Harvey.

Harvey who?

I hope you Harvey very

good sleep.

Goodnight!

Knock knock.
Who's there?
A little old lady.
A little old lady who?
**I didn't know you went
to yodelling school!**

Knock knock.
Who's there?
Artichokes.
Artichokes who?
**Artichokes when he
eats too quickly!**

Knock knock.

Who's there?

Omelette.

Omelette who?

Omelette ing you come to my party if you open the door!

Knock knock.

Who's there?

Dewey.

Dewey who?

Dewey have to go to school tomorrow? My favorite band is in town!

Knock knock.

Who's there?

Annette.

Annette who?

The best way to catch a fish is with Annette! Let's go fishing!

Knock knock.

Who's there?

Ben.

Ben who?

Ben knocking so long I forgot why I'm here!

Knock knock.

Who's there?

Accordion.

Accordion who?

Accordion to the radio, it's about to rain!

Knock knock.

Who's there?

Gopher.

Gopher who?

Gopher help quick! I think I broke my leg! Owwww!

Knock knock.
Who's there?
Athena.
Athena who?
Athena bear in your house so RUN!!!!!

Knock knock.
Who's there?
Alaska.
Alaska who?
Alaska when I see her! Should be next week!

Laugh Out Loud
Q & A Jokes!

How do you know if a hippo has been living in your refrigerator?

There are footprints in the butter!

What do Cannibals call athletes?

Fast Food!

Why didn't the moon finish its dinner?

It was full!

Where do bees go for a holiday?
Stingapore!

Which type of fish swims at night?
A starfish!

Why did the butcher become
a policeman?
So he could do a steak out!

What did the doctor say to the patient who thought he was a goat?
How are the kids?

What do you call a really big cat with big teeth that lives next door?
A neighbor toothed tiger!

What did the digital clock say to his mom?
Look Mom, no hands!

How do prisoners in jail talk to their friends?

On their cell phones!

Why did the sheep get a ticket from the policeman?

She made an illegal ewe turn!

What did the potato chip say to the biscuit?

Let's go for a dip!

Why was the boy's report card wet?
**All the grades were below
C level!**

Where do baby pigs live?
In their playpen!

What did Santa do in his
vegetable patch?
Hoe, Hoe, Hoe!

What do you call a boy named Lee sitting by himself?
Lonely! (Lone Lee)

What do you call a girl giving a boy a piggyback?
Carrie!

What do you call a boy giving a girl a piggyback?
Carter!

Why did the musician strawberries meet up?
To have a jam session!

What's a fortune teller's favorite type of tree?
Palms!

Which vegetable gets served in jail?
Cell-ery!

Where do the friendly horses live?
In your neigh-borhood!

What did the doctor say to the patient
who thought he was a bell?
**If it persists for a week give
me a ring!**

Which dinosaur spoke English
and knew all the words?
The Thesaurus!

What do you call 6 security guards
at the Samsung shop?
Guardians of the Galaxy!

If a butcher is 6 feet tall and has big feet what does he weigh?
Meat!

Why did the rooster stop crossing the road?
He was too chicken!

What do you call a crazy loaf of bread?
A weir-dough!

What did the doctor say to the patient who was sick for the first 30 minutes every morning?
Get up half an hour later!

Why was the astronaut such a good cook?
His food was out of this world!

How can you see a leopard at night?
Use a spotlight!

What do you call a bee that complains all day?
A grumble bee!

Which dinosaur lifted heavy weights at the gym?
The Tyrannosaurus Pecs!

Why was the guitar a bit stressed?
He was highly strung!

What do you call a woman who puts her bills in the fire?

Bernadette! (Burn a debt)

What did the puppy say when he sat on sandpaper?

Ruff!

What did the doctor give the sick snowman?

Chill pills!

How did the dog stop the video from playing?
By pressing the paws button!

What happened when the cleaner slipped on the floor?
He kicked the bucket!

Why was the boxer so funny?
He always had a great punch line!

Crazy
Knock Knock Jokes!

Knock knock.

Who's there?

Arthur.

Arthur who?

**Arthur any leftovers from lunch?
I'm really hungry!**

Knock knock.

Who's there?

Canoe.

Canoe who?

Canoe help me fix my flat tire?

Knock knock.

Who's there?

CD.

CD who?

CD car out the front?

That's my new car!

Woo Hoo!

Knock knock.

Who's there?

Colin.

Colin who?

Colin all cars! Colin all cars!

Emergency!

Knock knock.
Who's there?
Hammond.
Hammond who?
Hammond eggs on toast!
Yummy!

Knock knock.
Who's there?
Alden.
Alden who?
When you're Alden with your
homework let's go fishing!

Knock knock.

Who's there?

Ammonia.

Ammonia who?

**Ammonia short person so
I can't reach the bell!**

Knock knock.

Who's there?

Fiddle.

Fiddle who?

**Fiddle make you happy
I'll keep telling jokes!**

Knock knock.
Who's there?
Jupiter.
Jupiter who?
Jupiter invite in my letterbox?
It looks like your writing.

Knock knock.
Who's there?
Armageddon.
Armageddon who?
Armageddon outta here!
Goodbye!

Knock knock.

Who's there?

Justin.

Justin who?

Justin case I forget my key can you leave it out for me?

Knock knock.

Who's there?

King Tut.

King Tut who?

King Tut key fried chicken for dinner tonight!

Knock knock.

Who's there?

Carmen.

Carmen who?

**Carmen get your candy!
Candy for sale!
Great prices!**

Knock knock.

Who's there?

Panther.

Panther who?

**My Panther falling down!
Noooo!**

Knock knock.

Who's there?

Dale.

Dale who?

Dale be comin' 'round the mountain when dey come!

Knock knock.

Who's there?

Al.

Al who?

Al tell you if you open this door and let me in!

Knock knock.

Who's there?

Buster.

Buster who?

I'm catching the Buster school tomorrow. How about you?

Knock knock.

Who's there?

Chicken.

Chicken who?

I'm chicken under the mat and I can't find the key! Noooo!

Knock knock.
Who's there?
Ancient.
Ancient who?
Ancient going to let me in?
I'm late for dinner!

Knock knock.
Who's there?
Emma.
Emma who?
Emma very hungry!
What's for lunch?

Knock knock.
Who's there?
Amin.
Amin who?
Amin already so don't worry about the door!

Knock knock.
Who's there?
Alby.
Alby who?
Alby back in 2 hours. Wait here please!

Knock knock.

Who's there?

Olive.

Olive who?

**Olive here but I forgot my key!
Nooooo!**

Knock knock.

Who's there?

Jess.

Jess who?

**Jess let me in please!
It's cold out here!**

Knock knock.

Who's there?

Felix.

Felix who?

Felix my ice cream one more time he can buy me a new one!

Knock knock.

Who's there?

Carla.

Carla who?

Can you Carla taxi for me please?

Thank you so much!

Ridiculous Q & A Jokes!

What do you call a lying snowman?
A snow fake!

When the buffalo was leaving to go to work, what did he say to his son?
Bison! (bye son!)

What did the 2 cats do after a fight?
Hiss and make up!

What do you call a stick of dynamite
that comes back when you
throw it away?
A BOOMerang!

How did the swim team get to practice?
They carpooled!

What do you call a robber who
only steals meat?
A hamburglar!

What is the funniest part of the day?
The laughternoon!

Why do vampires take so much
cough medicine?
To stop their coffin!

What did the doctor say to the patient
who thought he was a fish?
Just hop on these scales!

Why did Mickey Mouse join NASA?
He wanted to visit Pluto!

What do you call a boy with a calculator in his pocket?
Smarty Pants!

Why don't starfish take a bath?
They wash up on the shore!

Why was the fox in trouble?
He had a brush with the law!

How much does it cost a pirate
to buy corn?
A buccaneer! (A buck an ear)

What do you call the knees of
a baby goat?
Kidneys!

What do you call a ship that has sunk and shivers on the bottom of the sea?
A nervous wreck!

What did the cloud wear underneath his raincoat?
Thunderpants!

What is the quietest dog in the world?
A hush puppy!

What did the doctor say to the patient who thought he was a cell phone? **If it persists for 3 days give me a call!**

Why did the toilet go to hospital? **It was feeling flushed!**

What did the astronaut find in his frying pan? **An unidentified frying object!**

Which animal works at the bank?
The loan wolf!

What is Santa's cat called?
Santa Claws!

What do you call two guys with no
arms and legs hanging above
the window?
Curt and Rod! (Curtain Rod)

If a lion ate a clown how would he feel?
A bit funny!

Why are triangles good at
playing basketball?
They get three pointers!

Why was the artist so famous?
She sure could draw crowds!

Why did the vampire get in big trouble at the blood bank?
He was drinking on the job!

What did the fireman name his twin sons?
José and Hose-B!

What do you call a fish with no eyes?
Fsh!

What do cows look at in
the museum?
The Mooona Lisa!

Where is Dracula's office?
The Vampire State Building!

What is the proper name for a
dinosaur in high heels?
My-Feet-Are-Really-Saurus!

What was the ghost's favorite ride at the playground?
The ScaryGoRound!

What game did the Brontosaurus play with the caveman?
Squash!

What game do tornadoes play at parties?
Twister!

What is a cat's favorite car?
CAT-illacs!

What is small, round, white, lives in a jar and giggles?
A tickled onion!

Why was the boy sad when he ran out of cola?
It was soda pressing!

Silly
Knock Knock Jokes!

Knock knock.

Who's there?

Claire.

Claire who?

**Claire the way!
I need to use the bathroom!
Quickly!**

Knock knock.

Who's there?

Alpaca.

Alpaca who?

**Alpaca my bags in the morning
and be on my way!**

Knock knock.
Who's there?
Carlotta.
Carlotta who?
Carlotta trouble when it breaks down!

Knock knock.
Who's there?
Courtney.
Courtney who?
Courtney good movies lately?

Knock knock.
Who's there?
Amarillo.
Amarillo who?
Amarillo nice guy!
Just ask me!

Knock knock.
Who's there?
Abby.
Abby who?
Abby New Year!
Let's celebrate!

Knock knock.
Who's there?
Harley.
Harley who?
Harley ever see you nowadays!
How are the kids?

Knock knock.
Who's there?
Ash.
Ash who?
Bless you!
Would you like a tissue?

Knock knock.
Who's there?
Hacienda.
Hacienda who?
Hacienda the story!
Time for bed!

Goodnight!
Knock knock.
Who's there?
Dish.
Dish who?
Dish is a very nice house
you have here!

Knock knock.

Who's there?

Bacon.

Bacon who?

I'm bacon a cake for your birthday!
Do you want chocolate or banana cake?

Knock knock.

Who's there?

Figs.

Figs who?

Figs the bell please, this knocking is so last year!

Knock knock.

Who's there?

Betty.

Betty who?

Betty you can't guess how many times I have knocked on this door? 27 times!

Knock knock.

Who's there?

Cupid.

Cupid who?

Cupid quiet!
I'm trying to sleep here!

Knock knock.

Who's there?

Honeydew.

Honeydew who?

Honeydew you want to hear lots more jokes?

Knock knock.

Who's there?

Cook Who Cook.

Cook Who Cook who?

Are you a cuckoo clock?

Knock knock.

Who's there?

Barbara.

Barbara who?

Barbara black sheep, have you any wool?

Knock knock.

Who's there?

Daisy.

Daisy who?

Daisy me running but 'dey can't catch me!

Knock knock.
Who's there?
Pudding.
Pudding who?
**I'm pudding on my best
tie for dinner!
Do you like it?**

Knock knock.
Who's there?
Gerald.
Gerald who?
**It's Gerald friend from school!
Don't you recognize me?**

Knock knock.
Who's there?
Alex.
Alex who?
**Alex plain it all to you
in a minute!
Let me in!**

Knock knock.
Who's there?
Phil.
Phil who?
**Phil the car please.
We're low on gas!**

Knock knock.

Who's there?

Ken.

Ken who?

Ken I please have a drink? I am so thirsty!

Knock knock.

Who's there?

Lucy.

Lucy who?

Lucy lastic and your pants fall down!

Knock knock.

Who's there?

Dexter.

Dexter who?

Dexter halls with boughs of holly!

Knock knock.

Who's there?

Baby owl.

Baby owl who?

Baby owl see you at school next week!

Bonus
Q & A Jokes!

Which piece of a computer is
an alien's favorite?
The space bar!

What do you call a cat who
ate a lemon?
A sourpuss!

What did the can of soda study
at college?
Fizzics!

Why did the boy bury his radio?
The batteries were dead!

Which superhero loves
clam chowder?
Soup-erman!

Why was the alligator using a
magnifying glass?
He was an investigator!

What did the skeleton order
at the restaurant?

A glass of water and a mop!

Why didn't the boy like the wooden
car with the wooden engine.

It wooden go!

Where do geologists go on
Saturday night?

Rock concerts!

Why did the meteorologist have
a day off?
He was a bit under the weather!

What should you eat if you have
a cold?
Maccaroni and Sneeze!

What kind of cat is no fun to
play a game with?
The cheetah!

Why did the caterpillar go to the party?
He was a social butterfly!

What is a nut with facial hair called?
A mustachio!

How long do Math Teachers live for?
Until their number is up!

What fish would never bite a woman?
A man eating shark!

What do you get if you dive into
the Red Sea?
Wet!

Why did the cowboy look exactly the
same as the other cowboy?
He was the Clone Ranger!

What happened to the witch
who cheated at school?
She was ex-spelled!

What are two rows of vegetables called?
A dual cabbage way!

What did the boy say when his dad
took a skunk on their vacation?
This holiday stinks!

Where did the car go for a
morning swim?
The carpool!

What are 2 birds in love called?
Tweet hearts!

What do dogs love to eat for breakfast?
Pooched eggs!

Why did Humpty Dumpty love autumn so much?
He had a great fall!

What roads do ghosts like to haunt?
Dead ends!

What do you call a cow in a washing machine?
A milkshake!

What do you call a boy with
no money?
Nickel-less! (Nicholas)

Why didn't the shark eat the man
in the submarine?
He didn't like canned food!

What did the rude young dinosaur
call his old granddad?
An old fossil!

What time is it when an elephant
sits on your lunch box?

Time to get a new lunch box!

Why did the dustpan marry
the broom?

She was swept off her feet!

What did the doctor say to the patient
who thought he was a cat?

How are the kittens?

Which animal appears on
legal documents?
A seal!

What do clocks do every day
after lunch?
They go back four seconds!

What did the germ wear after a bath?
A Mic-robe!

Where does Superman buy
his toothpaste?
The supermarket!

What did one tonsil say to the other?
**Better get dressed.
We're going out tonight!**

How do you get a spaceman's
baby to sleep?
Rocket!

Bonus Knock Knock Jokes!

Knock knock.

Who's there?

Design.

Design who?

Design says you are open for lunch! I'm hungry!

Knock knock.

Who's there?

Barbie.

Barbie who?

Barbie Q Chicken for dinner? Yummy!

Knock knock.

Who's there?

Fangs.

Fangs who?

Fangs for letting me come to your party. It's gonna be fun!

Knock knock.

Who's there?

Army.

Army who?

Army and you still going to the movies?

Knock knock.

Who's there?

Hamish.

Hamish who?

Hamish you so much when I don't see you!

Knock knock.

Who's there?

Delta.

Delta who?

Delta great hand in a card game last night!

Knock knock.

Who's there?

Des.

Des who?

Des no way I can reach the bell! Help!

Knock knock.

Who's there?

Kim.

Kim who?

Kim here and give me a kiss. I have missed you so much!

Knock knock.
Who's there?
Elsa.
Elsa who?
**Who Elsa do you think it would be?
Let me in!**

Knock knock.
Who's there?
Candice.
Candice who?
Candice bell actually ring because I have pressed it 22 times!

Knock knock.

Who's there?

Adam.

Adam who?

If you Adam up I'll pay half the bill!

Knock knock.

Who's there?

Ahmed.

Ahmed who?

Ahmed a mistake!
Sorry!
Wrong house!

Knock knock.
Who's there?
Art.
Art who?
r2 d2!

Knock knock.
Who's there?
Adair.
Adair who?
Adair when I was younger but now I'm bald!

Knock knock.

Who's there?

Funnel.

Funnel who?

Funnel start in just a minute! Woohoo!

Knock knock.

Who's there?

Dora.

Dora who?

Dora's locked so should I climb through the window?

Knock knock.

Who's there?

Garden.

Garden who?

Garden the treasure chest from the pirates. Aarrrrrr!

Knock knock.

Who's there?

Annie.

Annie who?

Annie body home? I've bought you a present!

Knock knock.
Who's there?
Jamaica.
Jamaica who?
Jamaica big mistake by answering the door! This is the Police! Hands up!

Knock knock.
Who's there?
Early Tibet.
Early Tibet who?
Early Tibet and early to rise!

Knock knock.
Who's there?
Doris.
Doris who?
Doris a bit squeaky!
I think you need to oil it!

Knock knock.
Who's there?
Butcher.
Butcher who?
Butcher right leg in,
Butcher right leg out...!

Knock knock.

Who's there?

Disguise.

Disguise who?

Disguise the limit!

Knock knock.

Who's there?

Honey Bee.

Honey Bee who?

Honey Bee kind and open the door for your grandma!

Thank you!

.... so much for reading our book.

We hope you had lots of laughs and enjoyed these funny jokes.

We would appreciate it so much if you could leave us a review on Amazon. Reviews make a big difference and we appreciate your support. Thank you!

Our Joke Books are available as a series for all ages from 6-12.

To see our range of books or leave a review anytime please go to FreddyFrost.com.

Thanks again!

Freddy Frost

Printed in Poland
by Amazon Fulfillment
Poland Sp. z o.o., Wrocław

64890701R00063